This Little Tiger book belongs to:

For Andrea and Jude ~ CR

LITTLE TIGER PRESS An imprint of Magi Publications

1 The Coda Centre, 189 Munster Road, London SW6 6AW

www.littletigerpress.com

First published in Great Britain 2008

This edition published 2009

Text and illustrations copyright © Catherine Rayner 2008

Catherine Rayner has asserted her right to be identified as the author and illustrator of this work under the

Copyright, Designs and Patents Act, 1988

Printed in China • LTP/1800/0240/0311

10 9 8 7 6 5

HARRIS FINDS HIS FEET

CATHERINE RAYNER

LITTLE TIGER PRESS
London

Harris was a very small
hare with very big feet.

"Why do I have such enormous feet,
   Grandad?" Harris sighed.

"All hares have big feet,
   young Harris," said Grandad
   with a whiskery smile.
"I'll show you why."

Grandad hopped high into the sky.

Harris copied.
His small, clumsy bounces
grew bigger . . .

and better . . .

and higher . . .

until he could spring,
like Grandad, into the air.

Then Grandad took
Harris up, up, up to the
very tops of the mountains.

"With your strong feet," he said,
"you can hop to the top of the world . . ."

"... and look out whe

e birds fly, as the wind tickles your whiskers."

Grandad showed Harris all the best things.
Like how to dig a cool resting place in the
earth when the days were hot.

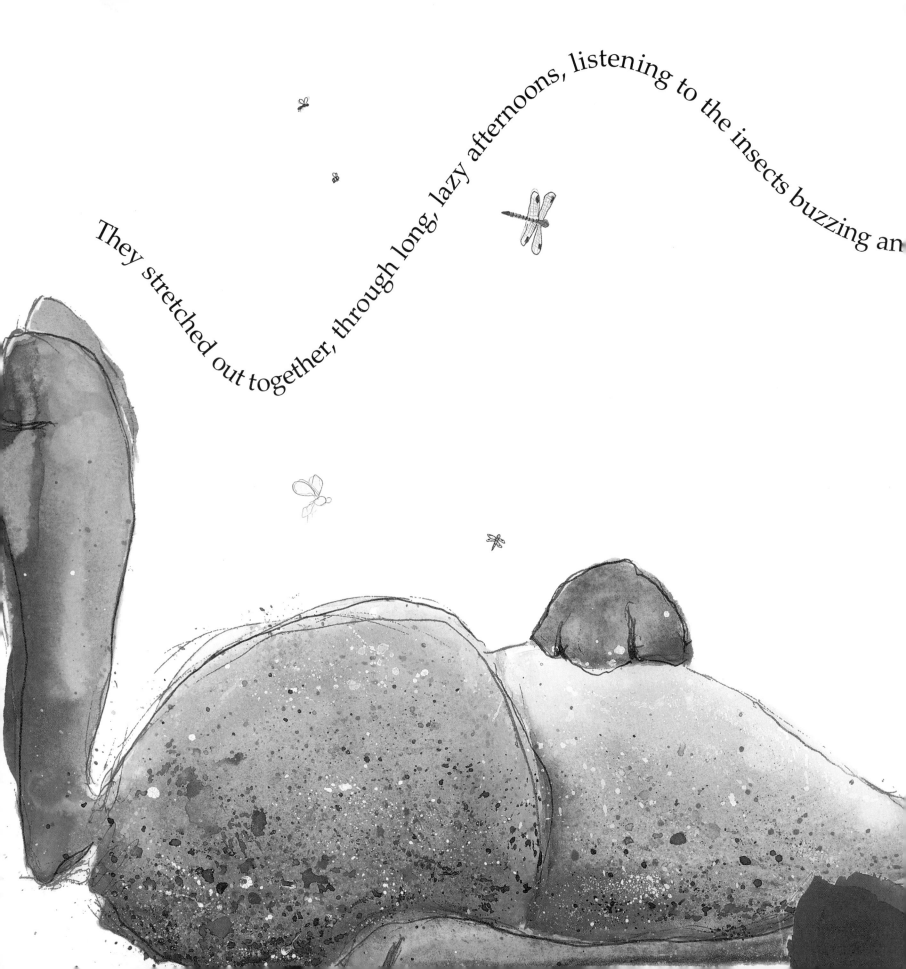

They stretched out together, through long, lazy afternoons, listening to the insects buzzing an umming around them.

"Look, Grandad!" Harris said. "My feet
can shade me from the sun!"

Every day Harris learned more about his world.

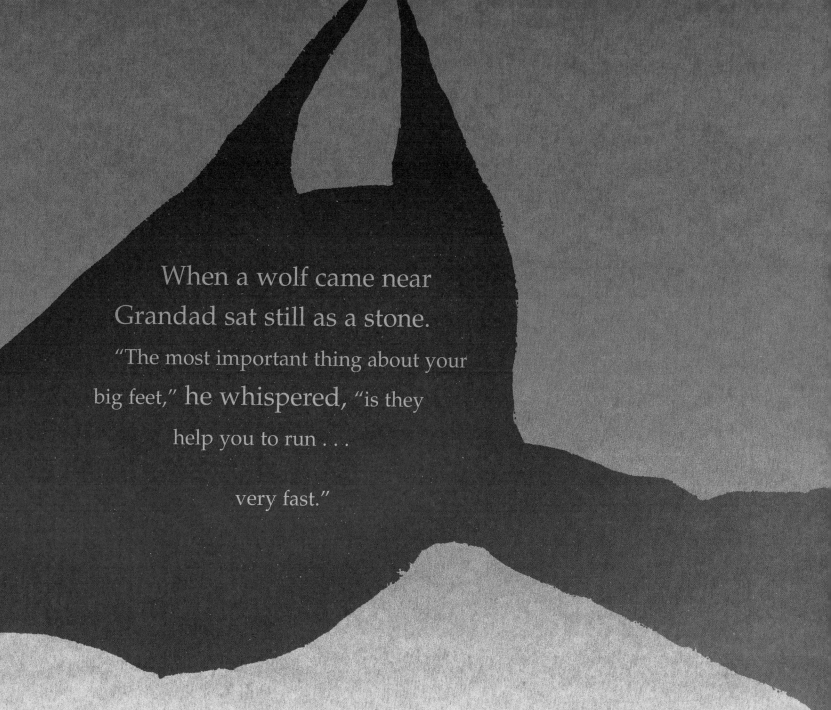

When a wolf came near
Grandad sat still as a stone.
"The most important thing about your
big feet," he whispered, "is they
help you to run . . .

very fast."

So Harris ran, feeling the bounce in his feet
and the stretch in his legs.

He ran faster and faster . . .

as fast as fast . . .

until . . .

. . . he was on his own.

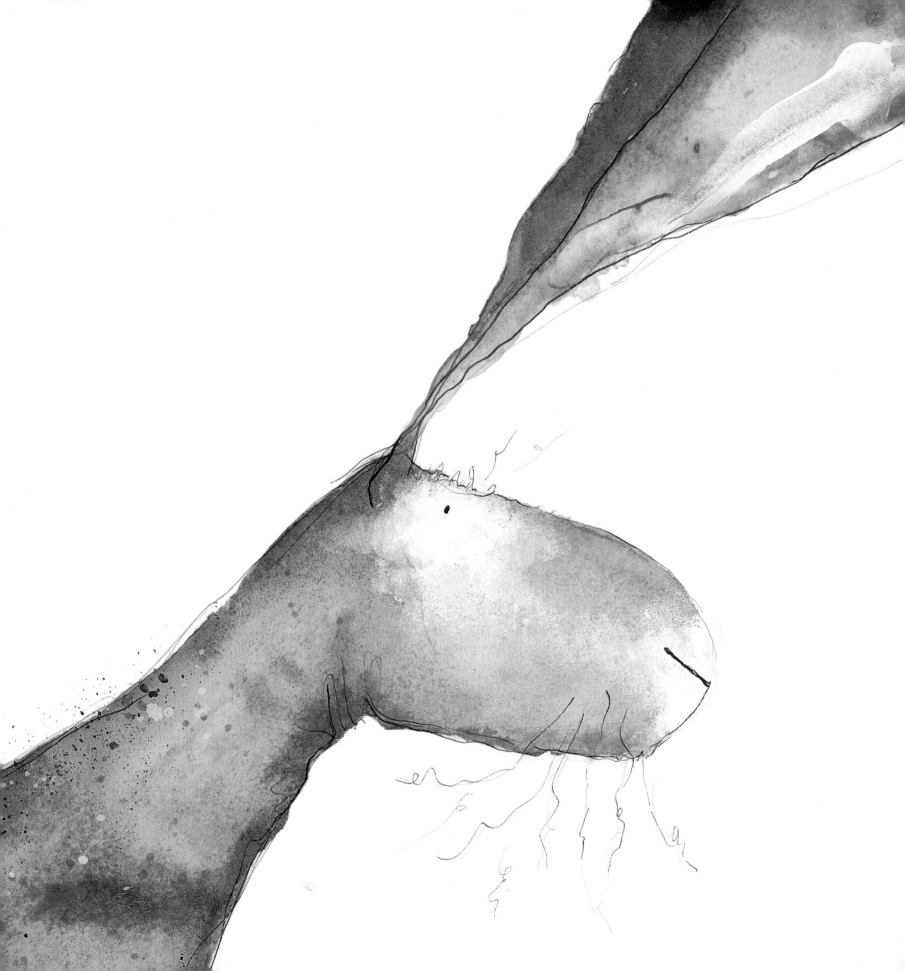

"Grandad!" Harris cried, hopping back. "Why aren't you running with me?"

"Because I'm growing old, little Harris. It's your turn to run. The world is yours to explore."

And Harris ran,
   leaping over streams
   and bouncing through meadows
on his big, strong feet that would take him
                to the end of the world . . .

                and back home again.